To Owen, with love T. K.

For Lucy J. M.

First published 2019 by Walker Books Ltd, 87 Vauxhall Walk, London SE11 5HJ

10 9 8 7 6 5 4 3 2 1

Text © 2019 Timothy Knapman

Illustrations © 2019 Jane McGuinness

The right of Timothy Knapman and Jane McGuinness to be identified as author and illustrator respectively
of this work has been asserted by them in accordance with the Copyright, Designs and Patents Act 1988

This book has been typeset in Quicksand

Printed in China

British Library Cataloguing in Publication Data: a catalogue record
for this book is available from the British Library

ISBN 978-1-4063-7687-6

www.walker.co.uk

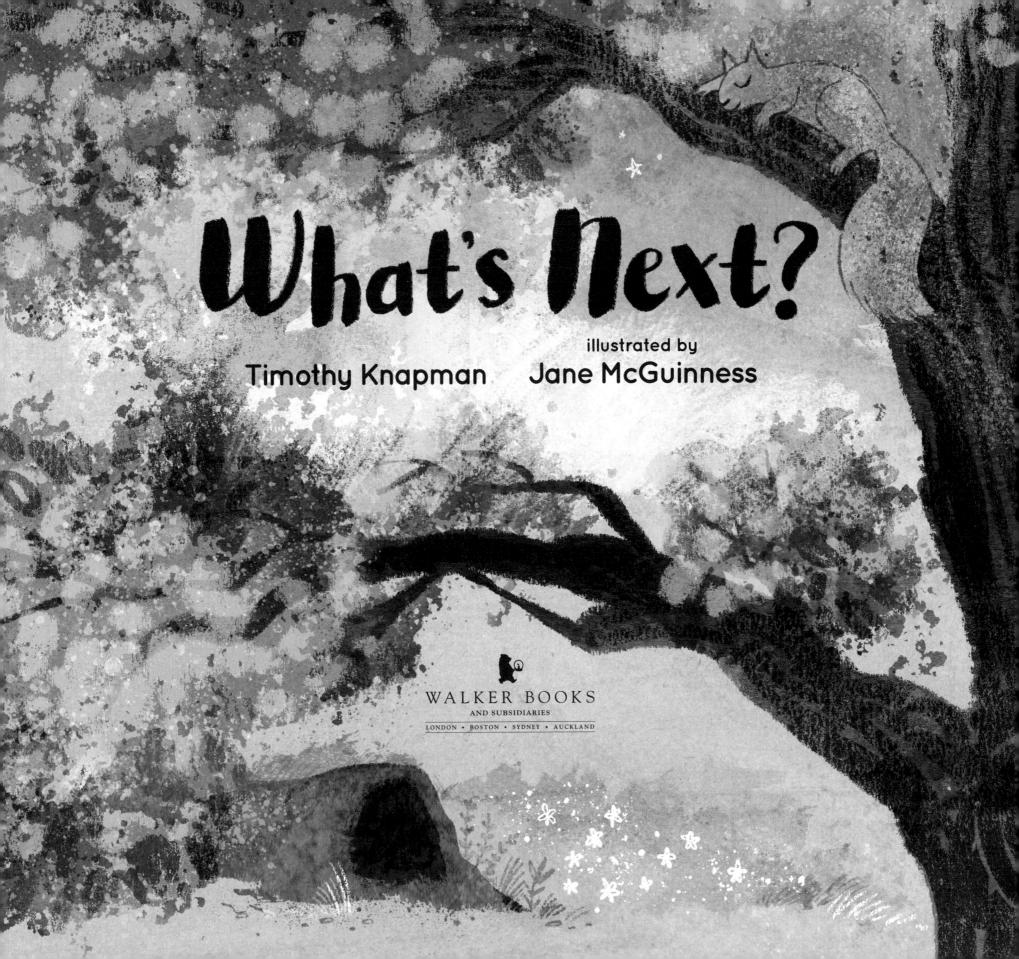

What's Next?

Timothy Knapman   illustrated by Jane McGuinness

WALKER BOOKS
AND SUBSIDIARIES
LONDON · BOSTON · SYDNEY · AUCKLAND

Baby Badger slept all day in the snuggly dark of his underground home, and woke up as night was falling.

The moment his eyes were open, he would go exploring.

Soon, he knew his underground home inside out.

And that's when Baby Badger said...

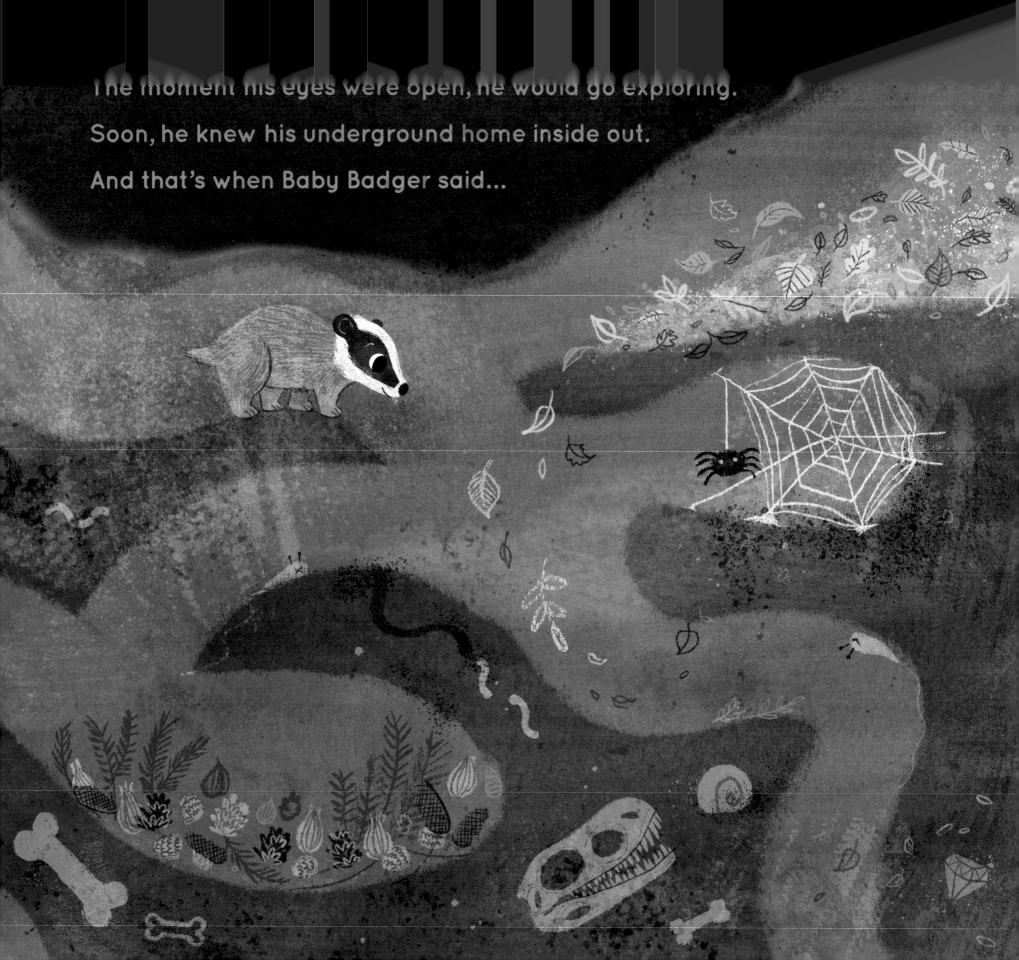

"What's next?"

"There's a whole forest up above us," said Daddy.

"Can we go exploring there as well?" said Baby Badger.

"Of course, my darling," said Daddy.

So the next night, Daddy took

Baby Badger to the forest up above.

Daddy showed Baby Badger the softest moss to roll in.

And Baby Badger said, "What's next?"

Daddy showed Baby Badger where to go snuffling for bluebell bulbs.

And Baby Badger said, "What's next?"

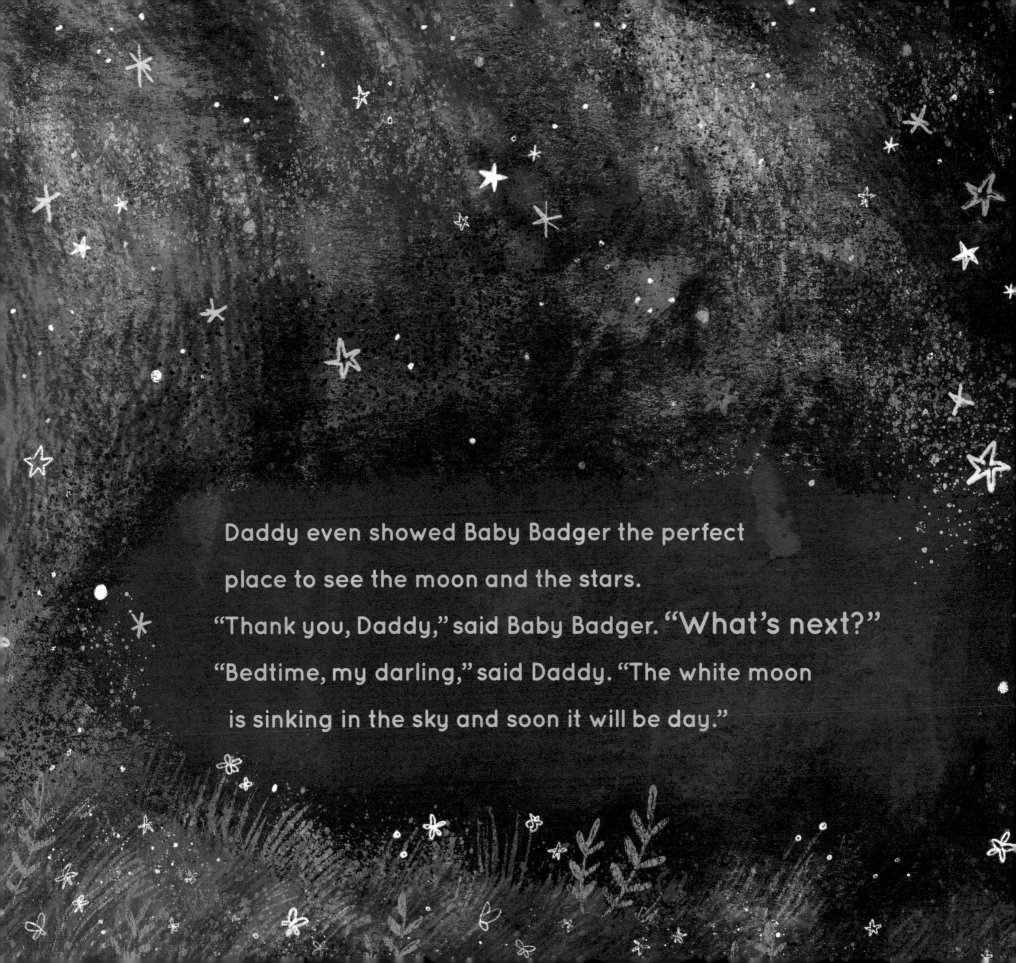

Daddy even showed Baby Badger the perfect
place to see the moon and the stars.

"Thank you, Daddy," said Baby Badger. "What's next?"

"Bedtime, my darling," said Daddy. "The white moon
is sinking in the sky and soon it will be day."

"So *day* is what's next," said Baby Badger as they walked home.

"What is day like?"

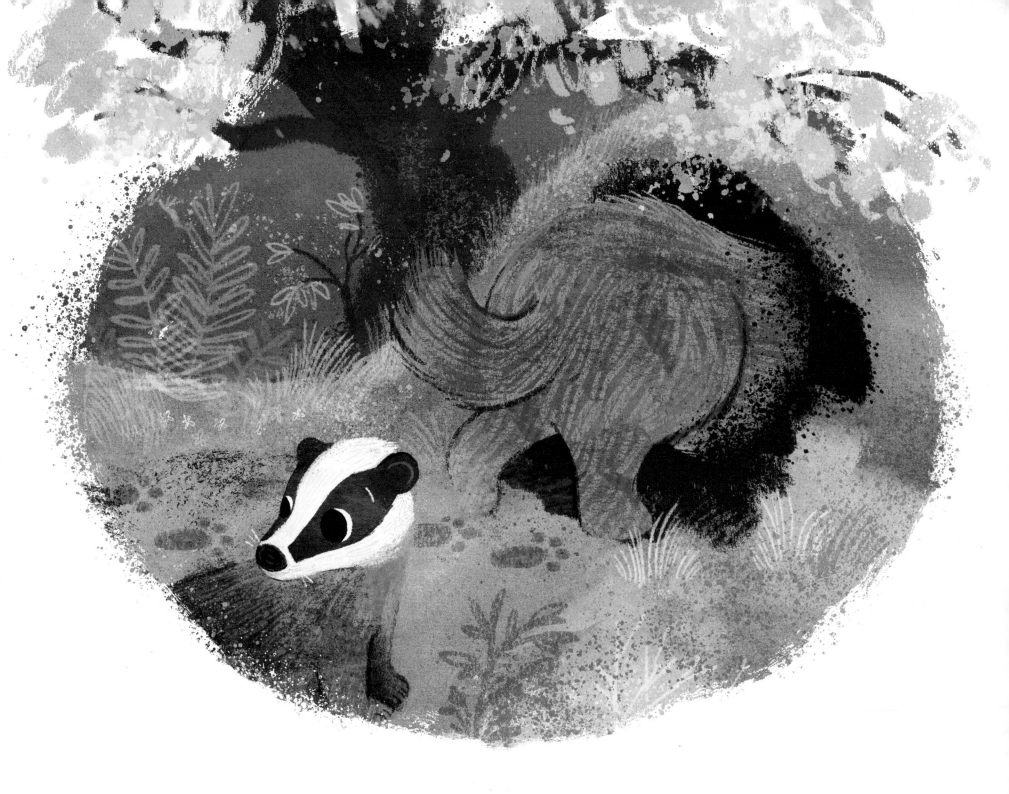

"It's a long time since I saw day," said Daddy. "I'm always fast asleep."

And that set Baby Badger wondering...

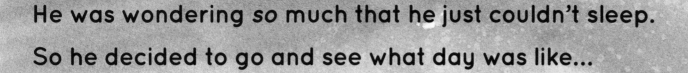

He was wondering *so* much that he just couldn't sleep.
So he decided to go and see what day was like...

Day smelt warm and fresh
and just-been-rained-on.
Baby Badger stepped out
of his burrow and into
a world of...

Green grass and orange flowers, red berries,

brown birds and purple butterflies!

"Oh my!" said Baby Badger, blinking. "This is what's next!"

It was like a whole different forest!

And Baby Badger went exploring.

He found the softest moss to roll in ... only now it was cosy green!

He found the bluebell bulbs ... only now they were bright blue!

He found their perfect place ... only now

he could see the yellow sun and the blue sky.

But the sun was very bright in his eyes and hot on his thick fur.

Baby Badger yawned. It was long past his bedtime

and he wanted to go home. But he didn't know how.

"What's next?" worried Baby Badger.

But there was nobody around to answer.

And that's when he saw...

"DADDY!"

"There you are, my darling!" said Daddy.

"What are you doing out of bed?"

"I wanted to know what's next," said Baby Badger.

"*I* know what's next," said Daddy.

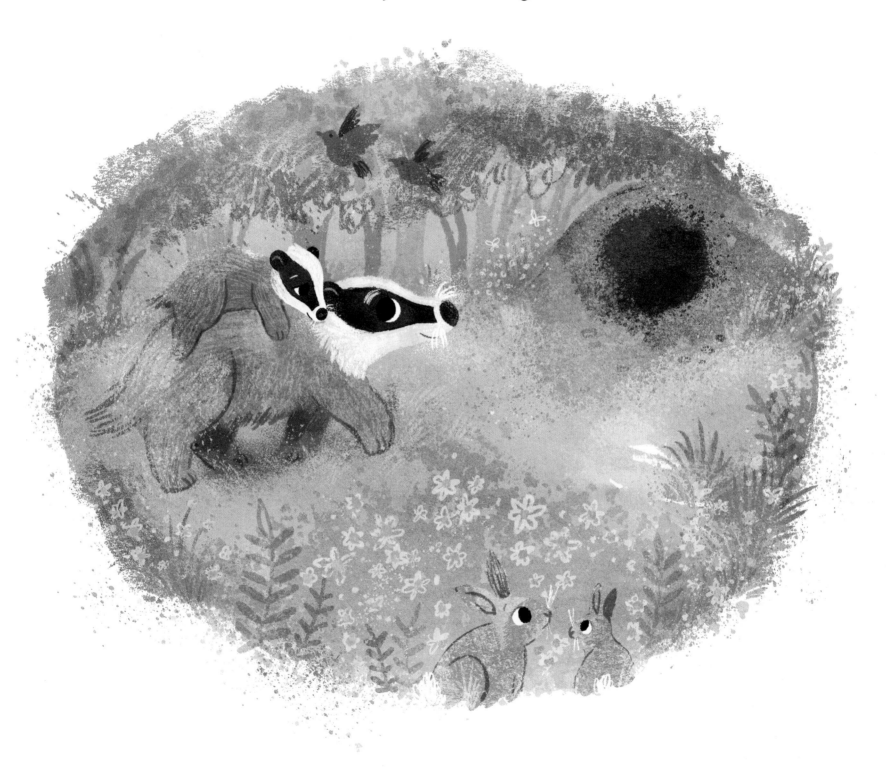

Sleep. Good night, my darling.
And Daddy Badger laid Baby Badger down in the
snuggly dark of his underground home ...

where everything was just right.